Lost in Time

Donna Shelton

SADDLEBACK
EDUCATIONAL PUBLISHING

MONARCH JUNGLE

SADDLEBACK
EDUCATIONAL PUBLISHING
www.sdlback.com

ISBN-13: 978-1-68021-478-9
ISBN-10: 1-68021-478-0
eBook: 978-1-63078-832-2

Printed in Guangzhou, China
NOR/1117/CA21701345

22 21 20 19 18   1 2 3 4 5

MONARCH
JUNGLE

Chapter 1

Give Me a Break

Being a responsible teenager has its pluses. Your parents trust you. They do things like buy you a car. Any teen would be happy about that. What you don't know is how long they've waited for this moment. Now you can drive your little sister places. That's what happened to me.

Today is Saturday. It's noon. But I'm still in my pj's. I settle in for a long session of texting. My best friend, Liv, broke up with her boyfriend. I've heard it all before. They've broken up three times.

She just sent me a long message. It's mostly about how mean Mark is. He controls everything Liv does. It makes me sad for her. I hope she leaves him for good this time.

I start to text when there's a knock on my door. I'm sure it's my sister, Teera.

"Go away! I'm busy!"

"Tansy?"

Oops. It's Mom.

"Can I come in?"

"Sure," I call out.

The door opens. Teera is there too. I know what this means. She wants to go somewhere.

"Your sister needs to go to the library."

I don't want to do it. But those were the rules when I got the car.

"Fine," I say.

"Don't be too long," Mom says. "Were having barbecue. Dad's making ribs."

Yum. I'm already hungry. Mom leaves the room. Teera stays behind.

"Will you help me with my book report?"

"What's it about?"

Teera looks at her notebook. "Wyatt Earp and the Cowboys," she reads.

"From the Old West? I saw a movie once. Wyatt Earp was a sheriff. And there was a gang of outlaws. They were called the Cowboys. That's all I know."

"Then just give me one of your old reports. I can copy it," she says,

"That's cheating. Besides, they're all on the Middle Ages. And sorcery. It's too scary for you."

"Ooh. You mean witches? Cool."

"You're not using my reports. Now get out, please. I need to get dressed."

My phone is going off again. I didn't answer Liv's text yet. And now she thinks I'm ignoring her.

"I'll meet you in the car!" I tell Teera.

Chapter 2

Bad Brakes

At the library, Teera wanders off down an aisle. I head for the young adult section. It's an awesome space. Big windows let in lots of light. And there are comfy sofas.

I find a spot and settle in. I start reading Liv's text. It starts out, "Boyfriend from hell." Liv was talking to a guy. Mark got jealous. He started a big fight. Then he told Liv that he was going to—.

"Tansy! Look what I found."

"Oh, good. You got a book. Let's go."

"I don't mean that." Teera shoves something in my face. It looks like a gemstone.

"Turn it in at the front desk. And check out that book if you're getting it."

Teera holds the stone up to the window. It catches the sunlight and glimmers. "It's so pretty. Can I keep it?"

"Whatever. Check out the book. And hurry. I'm hungry."

"Okay. But I'm keeping the stone."

A librarian comes up to us. She's dressed in black. Her hair is black too. "Be quiet!" she says. "Or you'll have to leave!" She walks away.

"Great," I say to Teera. "You nearly got us kicked out."

"She's an old witch."

"Teera! That is not nice."

♕

I'm pulling out of the parking lot. "Teera!" I call out. "I can hear your music! Turn it down!"

Teera takes off her earphones. "What?" The music stops.

Now she's saying something about the stone. Then I hear a buzz. It's Liv again. She's been blowing up my phone.

It's hard to focus on the road. I nearly run a red light. Mom and Dad cannot know about this.

Teera holds the stone up to the windshield. It catches the sun. Light bounces and blinds me for a second. I reach out and grab air. Finally I'm holding the stone.

Jeez. There goes my phone again. Then there is a loud noise. Someone is laying on their car horn.

Tires screech. There's a loud boom. Teera grabs my arm. Then there is only bright light. It surrounds us like a blanket.

Chapter 3

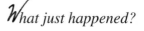

What just happened?

Pain jolts through my body. Every part of me hurts. Even if I wanted to move, I can't. It's nearly impossible to see or breathe. Panic is starting to set in.

I try to focus. How is Teera? I'm aware of her hand on my arm. But I can't tell if she's okay.

My hand is clasped around something sharp. Then I remember. It's the gemstone. It digs into my skin. I'm too frightened to care.

Moments pass. The loud noises start to fade. So does the light. Now everything is dark. I call out to Teera. "Are you okay?"

"Great," she sobs.

I should say something to comfort her. But my mind is blank. All I know is that we're trapped. And whatever happened? It's my fault. How could I have been so reckless?

There is a second of silence. Suddenly Teera lets go of me. "I can't see anything!" she cries. In a fit of anger, she punches my arm. "This is all your fault!"

"Hey!" I know she's scared. So am I. But I'm not going to sit here and let her hit me. "Don't put all the blame on me."

"You're so stupid! I can't believe that I'm related to you!"

Teera always tries to get in the last word.

"Just be quiet," I say. "You're wasting oxygen."

"What's the difference? We're going to die anyway. Unless we magically get out of here."

"We are not going to die," I tell her. "And we will get out of here." How? I don't know.

Chapter 4

Ready to Ride

Teera is quiet except for a few sighs. I let out a deep breath. My hand relaxes. The stone is still there. But instead of pain, I feel warmth.

I close my eyes for a moment. When I open them again, I see a faint white glow. It's coming from the stone.

"Look, Teera."

"I see it," she says.

The glow gets brighter. Soon it fills our small prison with light. There is enough to see each other's faces. In just seconds, the stone heats up in my hand. It burns me. But I can't let go.

I look at Teera. Her eyes are on the white-hot stone. Suddenly there's a flash of light. A gust of wind blows through. Its force sends us flying. We land with a thud.

"Whoa!" I hear Teera say. "That was weird."

I stand up and look around. Now where are we? And where is my phone?

Teera scrambles to her feet. "What is this place?"

"I'm not sure," I say. But it looks familiar to me. It seems to be a ranch. I think I've been here before. If I'm right, there are riding trails. I've taken lessons. My favorite horse is a red mare.

"There should be an office," I tell Teera. "We can call Mom and Dad."

We walk for about a mile. "Something isn't right," I finally say. There is no office. No riding trails. Not even one horse. Instead, there is desert. It stretches to the mountains.

Up ahead is a sign. As we get closer, I see what it says. Tombstone. It makes me think of the Old West.

Soon we come to the town. The streets are dry and dusty, which is made worse by the wind.

We pass tents where men are mining. Ahead is a main street lined with buildings. Along the way, we see horses. This is a good sign. Except these horses are tied to hitching posts.

A stagecoach flies by. Dust rises up and covers us. When it settles, we see all the people. Maybe they can help us. But then I see their clothes.

Men wear wool pants, long coats, and vests. Others

have on brightly colored shirts and boots with spurs. A few men wear aprons. They greet customers and sweep their porches. These must be shop owners.

It seems odd that no one wears denim. Not even the miners. Or were jeans invented later?

The women wear Victorian clothes. Even in this heat they are covered up. Long sleeves. Gloves. Hat *and* parasol.

A few women are in ruffled skirts that are knee-length. I know this is short for the times. Their petticoats show. They remind me of saloon girls.

As we walk along, I notice the businesses. Ice house. Opera house. Jail. Dry goods. Several saloons. I get it! This is a movie set.

Outside one saloon is a group of cowhands. One of them tips his hat at me. I give a little smile.

Where are the lights and the movie cameras?

Bad Boys

As we walk, people stare at us.

"Let's pick up the pace," I tell Teera. I want to get away from the crowd. The way people watch us and whisper makes me uneasy. Now I'm not so sure this is a movie set. It feels more like the real Old West.

"Cowboys are so cute," Teera says.

"Stop flirting," I tell her. "And call them cowhands, not cowboys. If I'm right, that's a bad word around here."

A group of men gets my attention. It's the red sashes they're wearing. These are the outlaws I told Teera about. They're known as the Cowboys.

We come to a saloon. Sounds filter through the doors. There's a buzz of talking and laughter. Someone plays a piano.

Outside the saloon there's a bench. Teera and I sit down to rest. She takes off the chain she's wearing.

"Give me the stone," Teera says.

I hand it to her, and she slides it onto the chain.

"Perfect," she says. "Who's going to wear it?"

"Go ahead," I say. "But it might burn a hole in your shirt. And your skin."

"You know what?" Teera says. "You're the oldest. You should wear it." She hands it back to me.

"So you admit that I'm in charge."

Teera gets up and looks through the saloon doors. "It's hot out here. Let's go inside."

"We are not going into a saloon," I say in a low voice.

"It sounds like people are having fun."

"Are you kidding? That's not a kid's party in there. They're drinking and gambling. And doing other bad stuff. Besides, you saw the looks we got on the street. Who knows what will happen in a bar."

"What's your point?"

She jumps up and heads through the doors. So much for being in charge. I follow her into the saloon. The room is cool and dark. I have to admit it feels good.

We are barely inside when everything gets quiet. I look around and see mostly men. There are a lot of guns in here. They put down their drinks and stop talking. Even the music has stopped.

A man sitting at the bar gets up. He staggers over to us. "What kind of people are you?" he slurs.

I smell booze on his breath. "Forget it," I say as I back away.

My eyes dart around the room. In one corner is a group of men. They're wearing red sashes! They've stopped their card game to look at us.

Teera leans close to me. "What's with the red belts?"

"It's like a uniform. These are the Cowboys."

"Yeah? So?"

"The outlaws I told you about. The ones you're doing the report on."

"So they steal and stuff?"

"Yeah."

Now Teera is headed for the bar. With my head down, I follow her. She sits on a stool. I sit down too. By now the music is playing again. People go back to their card games and drinking.

The bartender stops polishing the bar and steps over. He wears a white shirt, bowtie, and vest. His mustache is twirled on each side. I can tell right away. This man has pride in his bar and himself.

"What can I get for you ladies?"

"Root beer," Teera says.

"We'll just have water, please," I say. I'd buy us something. But we don't have the right kind of money.

He brings two glasses of water and sets them down. "You look like you could use some food."

"That's okay," I say. *I would love some food right now.*

He disappears for a minute. When he comes back, he's holding two plates. "It's not much," he says. "Just some ham and baked beans. But it'll hold you over."

"Thank you," I say. Teera and I practically attack the food.

"After this, you should move on." He's speaking in a low voice. "Those outlaws over there? They're bad news. I don't like how they're looking at you."

I look over at them. They're looking back. I don't want to know what they're thinking. I'm trying not to show fear.

Chapter 6

Don't Shoot

"You're scared, aren't you?" Teera says. Her voice is loud enough for others to hear.

"Quiet!" I say. "Don't call more attention to us. Drink your water and we'll go."

She stares into the glass. "It's yellow."

"You need liquid. Or do you want to die?"

"There's something floating in it."

"Fine, then! Don't drink it!"

Teera is right about the water. But I can't let her see it bothers me. I take a drink and swallow hard. It tastes nasty, but it's wet. That's all that matters. I slam the rest of it.

"Let's go." I stand up to leave. The room gets quiet again. We've got to get out of here.

Teera hops off her stool. We head for the door. That's

when a man enters the saloon. He's wearing a badge. This must be the sheriff. He walks over to the Cowboys.

They stop what they're doing. Some get to their feet. One of the Cowboys steps forward. He pulls his jacket back. I see a gun. "Well now," he says. "If it isn't Wyatt Earp."

I was right. This is the Old West. We're in Tombstone, Arizona. A gunfight could break out at any time. I take Teera by the arm and pull her along. We follow a few other people outside.

Sounds of fighting erupt from the saloon. Glass shatters. Tables and chairs crash. People yell and punch each other. Oddly, the music keeps playing. Suddenly a man comes flying through the doors.

As if making a wish, I touch the stone. "I could use a knight in shining armor right now."

I feel a warmth on my chest where the stone is. There's a bright flash of white light. The town of Tombstone is gone.

"Tansy?"

I don't believe this. We're standing in a meadow. Teera points to a river and runs for it. She reaches in and feels the water. Before I can check it, she's drinking from her hands. "It's clean," she calls out.

I kneel beside her. The water does look inviting. And

it can't be worse than that nasty yellow gunk. I take a drink. After a few gulps, I slow down. My stomach hurts. I splash my face and slump to the ground.

"What's wrong?" Teera asks.

What a dumb question. We're out in the middle of nowhere. We don't have a phone. What could be wrong? "Oh, nothing," I say.

"At least we can rest for a while."

Rest would be nice. A nap would be even better. I'm so tired. But I'm not about to close my eyes. First I need to know where we are.

After a few deep breaths, I force myself up. Teera makes a face. But she gets up too. I have no idea which way to go. So I pick a path at random. We start walking.

Chapter 7

Going Nowhere

As the sun starts to set, I feel nervous. Where will we spend the night?

After a while, we come to a forest. But now it's getting dark. I'm not sure we should go farther.

Teera tugs at my arm. She wants to keep going. I tell her to hold on. Who knows what creatures live in these woods. There could be a bear's den.

While there's still some light, I decide to check it out. The forest could be the best shelter we'll find.

We wander into the woods. Through the trees, I see an area with large rocks. If we hid behind them, we'd be out of view. I'm not sure who or what we're hiding from. But it's best to be safe. We settle in among the rocks.

"Maybe we should take turns sleeping," Teera says.

"Good idea. You go first."

"Why don't you go first," Teera says. She's looking out through the shadows. "I don't know if I can sleep. There are too many bugs."

"Don't be silly." At that moment, I see a large spider behind her. "There's nothing to worry about."

"Still, I'm not all that tired," Teera says. "And you look wiped out."

"Are you sure? I can be asleep in two minutes." I lean against the rock. "We'll look for food in the morning."

"I hope we won't have to kill it."

"Better we kill it than the other way around."

Teera leans back too. I rest my head on her shoulder. The next thing I know, I wake to the sound of something moving. Teera half opens her eyes. Then she drifts back to sleep.

I stand and stretch. It's still dark. But beams of moon-light shine through the trees. It looks like the forest is glowing.

I'm looking around in awe. Then I think I see something. It's a figure. Or am I dreaming?

Chapter 8

Who Goes There?

"Hold!" a man's voice says.

I run back behind a rock and peek out. I can't see anything. So I venture out for a better look.

All is quiet. But I've found something. One of the boulders in our shelter is a small cave. This would make a good fort. Before I can look inside, Teera runs up behind me. She grabs my arm.

"You left me," she whines.

"I went 10 feet away."

"I heard voices."

"You're dreaming." I say this so I don't scare her. But then a horse whinnies.

Teera starts to walk away. I grab her arm. "Where are you going? I thought you were scared."

"I want to see what it is."

She jerks from my grasp, but I get ahold of her again.

"No," I say. "You stay here. I'll go."

"Stop bossing me around."

"Remember back in Tombstone? You said I'm in charge. Now stay here."

I creep out into the brush. Somewhere a fire is burning. Then I see horses. There are dozens of them.

Men are setting up camp. I notice their clothes. They're wearing long tunics and tights. All that's missing is the armor.

Suddenly I hear twigs snapping. Leaves crunch underfoot. Someone is running my way. I spin around, expecting to see Teera. Instead, I'm looking into a man's eyes. He's dressed in armor. His sword is pointed at me. My heart beats fast.

"Who are you?" he says with an accent. It sounds like he's from England.

"Tansy," I say.

He looks me over with a cold, icy stare. "Where is your weapon?"

I raise my hands to show I'm unarmed. That's when he lowers his sword. "Come with me."

Like a scared dog, I obey.

Oh, Lord!

My captor has me by the arm. He leads me through a camp. We pass men in tunics. Some sit in groups talking. Others are eating. There is an army of them and one of me. But they don't even look up.

I am led to a smaller group. They are sitting by a fire. A musician plays the flute. The men sit back and listen.

One man looks different from the others. His tunic is lined with gold trim. Across the tunic is a red shield. There are gold symbols on it. He also wears a cloak.

"My Lord. I found this maiden. She was hiding in the woods."

"A spy, Sir Devin?" The man stands up and comes over. He looks me up and down. "What is your name?"

"Tansy." Now I'm sure where the stone has brought

us. This lord is a ruler. And these men serve him. They are knights from the Middle Ages.

"What were you doing in the woods?"

"I heard noises. And I went to check it out."

He raises an eyebrow.

"I wasn't spying, I swear it. My sister and I are lost."

"Which county do you come from?"

"It's very far away," I say.

"Perhaps I can help. Where is this sister you speak of?"

"She's hiding in the forest. Please let me go. My sister is alone."

He leads me to a seat by the fire. "Do not be afraid," he says. "Neither my men nor I will harm you. Tonight you shall be guests in my camp. You will eat and rest."

He seems sincere. But I don't fully trust him. It must show because he takes my hand.

"I am Lord William. Ruler of this land. My knights will protect you. You have my word."

"Thank you. You are very kind." The idea of food and being warm and safe sounds good.

"Now you must find your sister. I will send Devin with you. In case you should run into trouble."

"What kind of trouble?"

"Wild boars," he says.

"The forest is full of them," Devin says. "They dwell in caves."

Caves? That gets my attention. "I left my sister near a cave."

A flood of scary images come to mind. I once read a news story about boars. They had mauled three people to death. Their bodies were torn to shreds.

"We must find your sister at once."

I nod to Devin and we leave the camp.

What a Boar

Devin walks ahead of me. His hand grips the handle of the sword at his side.

"Where are we?" I ask. "I mean besides the forest."

"The shire of Mares," he says in a low voice.

I know the word *shire*. "As in county," I say. "And mares as in horses?"

"Quite so," he says. "The finest horses are bred here."

"Sounds cool. I'd like to hear more about it."

"Are you cold, my lady?" He gives me his cape.

Cute! I'd love to send a selfie to Liv right now. If only I had my phone.

We come to the spot where I'd left Teera. She's nowhere in sight. "Teera!" I call out.

"Up here."

I look up at a nearby tree. Teera is sitting in the crook of the highest limbs.

"Are you okay?" I call.

"Boar!" Devin shouts as he holds out his sword.

I have never climbed a tree so fast. Actually, I'd never climbed a tree before.

The boar charges at Devin. He dodges to the side just in time. The beast turns and charges again. This time it catches Devin's leg with its tusks. He steps back then stabs at the beast. With a powerful stroke, it falls over, dead.

Teera and I climb down.

"Teera, this is Devin. He's a soldier."

She looks him up and down. "What kind of soldier?"

She's being rude. I give her a nudge.

"Let us return to camp," Devin says. He drags the boar behind him.

Teera and I hang back so we can talk. I quickly tell her what happened and what era we're in.

At camp, Devin drops the boar at the cook's station. The cook beams. "The men will be pleased," he says. "This will provide many meals."

Devin leads me and Teera to a tent. Since we are the only women, we will use his.

Before we go to bed, we eat something. It's just bread and cheese. But I'm so hungry. Most anything would taste good. But I do politely pass on the boar meat.

By now it's dark. Teera and I are curled up together on a cot.

"Are you awake, Tansy?"

"Yes."

"Remember when we were in Tombstone?"

"Uh-huh," I mumble.

"You made a wish. Then we came here."

"I remember."

"Can't we just wish to go home?" Her eyes close.

I already tried that. But I don't have the heart to tell her. "Go to sleep," I say.

Chapter 11

Good Knight

The next morning, I hear voices outside. I peek out from the tent and watch. Some of the knights practice using their weapons. Others eat breakfast or pray.

When Teera wakes up, she looks around. A frown comes over her face. I'm reading her mind. This hasn't all been a bad dream. We're still stuck back in time.

We step out of the tent. Judging by the sky, it's nearly sunrise. The camp is busy. Men are packing up.

Teera spots Devin. She runs his way. I hurry to catch up.

"Good morrow, ladies. Eat while you can. We will be leaving soon."

He waits as Teera and I pick out our breakfast. We get bread and honey. Then we all sit by the fire. Shortly after, Lord William comes over.

"Good morrow," he says.

Devin stands and bows. "My Lord."

Teera and I say hi.

"How did you sleep, ladies? Well, I hope," Lord William says.

"Yes," I answer. "Thank you."

"Very good. We will leave soon to continue west. Devin will find horses for you." He smiles and then vanishes into the camp.

After breakfast, Devin leads us to some horses. He chooses two. Mine is a red mare with a gray mane. Teera's horse is honey-colored.

"She's beautiful!" Teera gushes.

I've never seen my sister so happy. I hope she knows she can't keep it.

"You ladies stay here while I pack up."

As soon as Devin is out of sight, Teera turns to me. She seems excited. "I've changed my mind. I like it here. It's better than back home."

"We're not staying! Think about Mom and Dad. They're probably worried sick by now."

"But I've always wanted a horse. And Devin is so cute."

"He's too old for you."

"But you think he's cute. Right?"

"Maybe he's a little handsome. I haven't been paying attention." I turn to my horse and stroke its mane.

"Yeah, sure," Teera says.

I want to slap that smirk off her face. But she's right. Secretly, I do think Devin is cute.

The camp has been taken down by now. Soon there will be no sign we were ever here. Devin returns. He helps Teera and I mount our horses.

The knights set off side by side through the woods. Teera and I are in back with the supply wagons. That's when Devin comes galloping up. He's been assigned to guard us.

Soon we are clear of the woods. Now we are heading west. After hours of riding, my butt feels numb. Every few minutes, I glance at Teera. She has to feel the same way. If so I can't tell. A huge smile is on her face. It's like she's off in her own little world.

At least one of us is having fun.

Noble, Not

Devin rides beside me. Teera is just ahead of us. "Where are we going?" I ask him.

"To find Lord Merek of Dunsville."

"Who is that?"

"Merek is married to Lord William's sister. Her name is Olivia. She made friends with one of William's squires. Merek had him killed. In a rage, he put Olivia in prison. William plans to free her. First he must capture Merek. It is the only way to regain honor."

"So there's going to be a war?"

"We do not want bloodshed. Only that Marek pay for what he did. He must go to prison. If he does not cooperate, then we will fight. Marek will die or be hanged."

"What will happen to his castle?"

"Lord William will rule the land. And his kingdom will be richer."

He makes it sound like another day at the office.

"What will happen to me and my sister?"

"Lord William will protect you. You will work at one of his manors. Many consider it an honor."

"The offer is generous. But Teera and I need to get home."

"Where is home?"

He is waiting for an answer. But there's no easy way to explain. I can't even think of a good lie. We ride on for a few more miles.

"You did not answer my question," he says.

Just then Lord William calls us to a halt. We are to stop and rest, he says. There is a river here. The horses can drink.

Teera and I walk over to the meal tent. Again we have bread and cheese. Right now I would kill for a double iced mocha. We find a spot near the river and sit down.

"There's something weird about the men," Teera says. "Only Devin and Lord William talk to us. The others don't seem to know we're here. I wonder why."

"They're here to do a job. Not hang out."

Devin walks over to us and sits down. We eat in silence. When we're done, I ask Teera to check on our horses. I want to ask Devin about the upcoming battle. But when I mention it, he changes the subject.

"The stone you are wearing. It is quite unusual," he says. "I am curious to know about it."

"I don't know much. Just that it's magical."

Devin laughs. "So you are a witch? Do you plan to cast a spell on me? Maybe I should call for a priest. He can drive the devil out of you."

"No! I'm not a witch."

Seriously? Did I just mention magic? This is the Middle Ages. Witches were burned for that sort of thing. But I could be okay. It depends on the exact time period. At one point, the church taught that witches weren't real. Still, I wasn't taking chances. I'd have to explain.

"I come from the future," I say. An alarmed look comes over his face. This must have sounded even worse. But I'm in too deep to stop now. "Listen to the way I talk. And look at my clothes. Does it seem like I belong here?"

"Well, no. But how is this possible?"

"Teera and I found this stone. Then we started to travel back in time. I don't know how. But the stone got us here. Now I need to figure out how it works. Or we'll never get home."

Chapter 13

Ride or Die

"Then I am right," Devin says. "You are a witch."

It's no use. I shake my head. "No, I'm not. I swear it."

He stands up and begins pacing.

When Teera returns, she looks at me and then Devin. "What's up with him?"

"I told him about the stone. How it got us here."

Now Devin is staring at Teera. I see him looking at her hair. One side is long. The other side is shorter and shaved. "Is it true?" he asks her. "You are from the future?"

"It's true," she says.

I watch Devin as he paces. He seems to be deep in thought. Once in a while he looks over at us.

"What's going to happen?" Teera asks. "Is he going to tell the others?"

"They won't understand," I tell him. "Please don't say anything."

"I vow not to."

Devin sits down. He asks us many questions. I do my best to answer him. I'm not sure why I trust him. But somehow I know our secret is safe. Teera joins in until she sees a servant boy looking at her. She goes over to talk to him.

"Is your county anything like mine?" Devin asks me.

"Not at all. But I wish it was. I love everything about the Middle Ages."

"You can stay if you choose."

"But I have a home and a family. And I miss them." My mind wanders. I think of my parents. Suddenly I feel a deep sadness. It's a feeling that I'll never get home.

Devin is watching me. I can feel his gaze. Another question is coming. Before he can ask, I raise my hand. Then I look at him.

In that second, our eyes meet. He smiles and I smile back. I really like him. I'd like to get to know him better. What's his favorite color? What kind of music does he like? What does he do for fun?

Lord William's voice breaks through my thoughts. He is rallying the knights. I'm not sure if it's perfect timing or the worst.

Teera is waiting for us. She's already on her horse. I

notice the grin on her face. It's a look I've seen before. Next she'll say something to embarrass me.

I'll have to ward her off. I give her my best death stare. It works! The grin is gone. As we ride out, she is quiet. But for how long?

Our journey lasts nearly all day. It's just before sunset. We come up on a hill. Below is a city. A stone wall surrounds it. The iron gates are locked. Devin explains. Lord Merek's castle is inside. He knew we were coming.

I can see the castle. It towers high above the wall.

We head back to find a campsite.

As we set up, a boy rides in. He brings a message to Lord William.

"Lord Merek orders you to leave his land."

"Inform Merek of this," Lord William says. "I plan to arrest him for crimes against my people. He must surrender and give up his land by morning. If not, I shall burn down his city and take him by force."

The boy stands, bows, and jumps onto his horse. He vanishes behind a cloud of dust. Soon after, dark clouds roll in. Flashes of lightning fill the sky. Torrents of rain pour down on us. Not the nearby city. Just us. The men scatter for shelter.

Suddenly I realize I don't know where Teera is.

Devin pulls me into the tent. "This storm is the witch's doing," he says bitterly.

"There is a witch?" Now I'm nervous. Like being in the middle of a war isn't scary enough.

"Don't worry," he says. "I will protect you."

The rain continues to fall hard. I'm not too concerned about Teera. I know the knights will keep the camp safe.

Evil Times

Rain falls through the night. It finally lifts at sunrise. I'm surprised the tents held up. I was sure the camp would wash away.

I need to look for Teera. But first things first. I have to pee. When I step out of the tent, I see many of the men. They are busy cleaning the camp. Some shovel mud. Others clear out fallen branches.

I ride my horse to a spot beyond camp. Quickly I do my business and head back. All the talk of war and witches has me spooked.

Just then I hear wings flapping. A large crow flies over my head. It gives a loud caw. I nudge the horse with my heels. We take off at a fast trot. But I can't seem to escape the darn crow.

Its caws only get louder. Now they're coming closer.

I feel pain as claws scrape my face. Then I fall off the horse with a thud.

This time the crow dives at me. It digs its beak into my head. I let out a scream. The crow releases its hold. I fall flat on my back. It swoops down for another attack. I watch as its claws reach out. All I can do is brace for pain. Instead, I feel a tug at my neck. The stone is torn from me.

"Give it back!" I yell. I sit up and grab the stone. The struggle continues.

Suddenly there is a flash of light. A strong gust of wind knocks me over. The stone flies out of my hand.

I must have blacked out. I'm now in a dark room. The only light comes from a few candles. As my eyes adjust, I see creatures at my feet. Rats? Giant roaches?

Something smells bad. It's the odor of rotting meat. There is something or someone evil here.

Don't panic.

I feel around for a door. But that would be too easy. At that moment, laughter fills the room. It's like someone had read my mind.

An icy chill goes through me. The candles flicker in the dark. I'm frozen in fear.

A figure moves toward me. It casts odd shadows on the wall. What is it? Some kind of beast? An evil creature?

It steps from the shadows. I'm afraid to look. I cover my eyes. After a minute, I peek through my fingers. I see a woman.

She wears a long black dress. Jet black hair flows behind her. Then I see her face. It's white as chalk. Her eyes are big black pools. Scarlet red lips move to smile. I see jagged yellow teeth.

I feel like I might throw up.

She raises her fist to me. Clasped in her hand is my chain. The witch has the stone!

"Where did you get this?" she screeches.

My heart is pounding. But I try to hide my fear. "I found it," I say calmly. Inside, I'm shaking.

"This stone is magic," she says. "You are not worthy of its powers."

"I don't care about that. I just need it to get home."

"Which county would that be? One of Lord William's, I am sure."

"The 21st century."

"Quiet! I must think." She stares at the stone for a long while. Then she looks into my eyes.

"Do you know how old this is? It goes back to the beginning of time. It belonged to my ancestors. Their souls live inside. As do their powers."

None of this makes sense. Maybe I can reason with the old bag. "Look," I say. "I don't want any part of this.

War. An evil witch. Magic powers. It means nothing to me. I just want to find my sister and go home. The only way is with that stone."

She looks at me and laughs. It's more of a cackle, as you'd expect from a witch.

"Enjoy your new home," she says.

"Wait!" Before I can follow she's gone. The door locks behind her.

Like a child, I stomp my foot. "How am I supposed to get out of—"

The floor opens. There's no time to react. I'm falling fast. All I can do is wait for it to end.

The next thing I know I hit water like a rock. I should be in a million pieces. Maybe I am.

Now the current sweeps me away. There's nothing to grab on to. But I have no control anyway. Next I feel a sharp pain in my head. Then there is darkness.

Dead End

I wake to the sight of Teera. She sits beside me and holds my hand. There is a table beside my cot. Bottles are filled with oils and herbs. An old man stands over me. He dabs at my head with a cloth. This must be a doctor.

"Ow!" I cry in pain. It feels like fire. My head aches. "Do you have any aspirin?"

He gives me a puzzled look. "Whiskey is the best I can do."

As he leaves the room, Devin enters. I try to sit up. But my head is a lead weight.

"How did I get here?" I ask.

"Devin found you," Teera says. "You were by a river. Don't you remember?"

I tell them what I know. Teera panics when I say the stone is gone.

"It's our only way home!" she cries.

"We will get it back," Devin says. "The enemy will not win this war."

I hate to tell him. The witch has the stone. It's over. She has all the power.

"Why wait?" Teera says. "Let's go to the castle ourselves. We can go back the way you came, Tansy."

Devin takes my hand. "There is nothing we can do tonight. You must rest now."

The next morning, we go back to the river. The spot is along the wall to the city. There don't seem to be any guards around.

Devin takes a minute to assess the water. I probably would have just jumped in. He tosses a branch in to test the current. The branch barely moves. It should be safe. He takes off his shoes and steps in. The water is at his waist.

Teera and I take off our shoes. Devin offers us his hand and helps us in. It takes a second to adjust to the chill. Then we start walking in a line. I hold on to Devin. Teera holds on to me.

Soon we come to a tunnel. It's pitch black inside. We put our shoes on and feel our way through. The stone walls are cold and slimy.

After a while, the tunnel takes a turn. There is a faint light ahead. I see a door. It must lead into the castle. I go up to it and push. The door doesn't budge.

"Stand back," I say. I give the door a hard kick. Nothing happens. Epic fail.

Devin pulls me aside. He feels the door and finds a handle. Really? Who knew it would be that easy. I just smile as he holds the door open.

I'm not thinking ahead to what's inside. It just feels good to be out of the water. Devin and Teera look at me. "No! I am not leading the way."

Torches line the walls of a long hallway. They give off a warm amber glow. It's almost comforting. But I know there is evil here. Devin takes a torch down and sets off. Teera and I follow closely behind.

Pretty soon we come to a stairway. I stop and look up. My eyes follow the spiral to the very top. The sheer height and the flickering lights make me dizzy. Do we really want to do this?

The stairs creek under our feet. They don't feel too solid. I wonder if they can support our weight. The thought of falling again is more than I can take.

On the first landing there's a door. It is barred but not locked. Devin lifts the bar and pulls the door open. It leads to a hallway. We enter. When he shuts the door behind us, I look back. There is no way to open it. Who was being kept here? And why?

I feel myself being pulled along. It's like someone has me by the arm. Soon I'm in front of another door. Devin and

Teera are still down the hall. Before they can catch up, the door opens.

In a flash, I'm pulled inside. Then the door slams shut. The air is sucked from the room. A feeling comes over me. It's a sadness like I've never felt. This place is filled with suffering.

Fight it, I tell myself. *Don't let it get to you.*

But the force is too strong. I'm within its grip. My mind and my limbs are useless.

That's when I have a vision. Women are in the room. They huddle together and whisper. I notice some have bruises. Others have scars.

There are children here too. Many of them are crying. The images are so clear. It's like I'm with them. I can hear their thoughts.

We must get to the river. It is our only hope of freedom.

Now I know who the women are. They are the lowest class. The lord of the manor owns them. They are forced to serve. Escape is a dream. All that awaits them is death.

If I don't stop this vision, I'm sure I'll die too. I try to focus on what I know. Teera. My mom and dad. Liv, my best friend. We should be texting right now. She needs me. I see myself in my bedroom. I want so badly to be there.

Suddenly I'm aware of what's around me. It's not my bedroom. But the scary visions are gone. Air fills my lungs. I can breathe again.

Chapter 16

Cornered

After a few minutes, I leave the room. For now I seem to be out of danger. But where are Devin and Teera?

As I wait, I smell a bad odor. It reminds me of something. But what? Then it comes to me. The room where the witch held me! Someone touches my shoulder. I turn to look.

"Are you okay?" Teera says. "Where did you go?"

"You don't want to know." I point to a door. "This is the witch's chamber," I say.

Devin nods.

"I'll stand guard," Teera says.

Devin pulls a small dagger from his belt. He holds it out to me. I take it and slip it into my pocket.

"I'll lead the way," he says.

My knight in shining armor! Suddenly I find the

phrase both funny and annoying. It's what got me here in the first place.

The door creaks as Devin opens it. Then all is quiet. Too quiet. We step inside and close the door behind us. Except for a few candles burning, the room is dark.

"We must hurry," he whispers.

We start searching for the stone. I'm behind a drape when I hear the door open. I quickly crouch down. I'm not sure where Devin is.

Through the sheer fabric, I see a shadow on the wall. The witch opens a box. Then she lifts something out. She puts it around her neck. It's my chain! Just then she looks up.

"I sense a familiar soul." She takes a whiff of air. "Ah yes. The girl."

I'm shaking. Sweat runs down my face.

"I know you are here." Her voice is calm and gentle.

I cover my mouth to hold in a gasp.

"Did you come for the stone?" she asks.

I'm sure she can hear me breathe.

"I am losing patience. Show yourself now!"

She takes a few steps in my direction. My heart starts beating faster.

"All right, then. I will have to find you."

She strikes a match and lights a candle. I see her face in the glow. It's just as ugly as I remember. Now she moves toward me.

"Do not be afraid," she says. "I am not going to kill you. I would have already done so."

Only the drape separates us. She pulls it back. "Hello, Tansy. I have been waiting for you. The stone brought you here. There is much I have to share with you."

I fall on my butt and scoot backward. The witch sweeps her hand in a lifting motion. I feel myself rise and move across the room.

I'm standing in front of a table. On top is an object. It is covered with a cloth. She pulls it aside, and I see the glass ball. I quickly glance around the room. Devin has to be here somewhere.

Now the witch waves her hands over the ball. She chants in a strange language.

"You are part of me. I have seen it in my crystal ball. Look for yourself, Tansy. You will see the truth."

I know the truth. You are insane.

But then I see smoke. It swirls inside the ball. Faces fade in and out. Their eyes pull me in. There is something familiar about them.

Chapter 17

Bad Magic

"Look into their eyes," the witch says. "You know them. They are members of our family." Her voice is soothing. It lulls me into a trance.

I've lost all sense of the present. My eyes focus on the images in the ball. Then I see my grandma. And there's Mom and Dad! And Teera as a baby! Me as a toddler! Then I see the witch's face. I quickly look away.

"That's right. I am your family. The stone brought you back to me. And now it is mine again. All my powers are restored."

She moves her hands away from the ball. The smoke fades.

"You can't keep me here."

"Do you really think I will let you go? There is too

much to lose. There is a way this can work for both of us. I am thinking of sharing the stone with you."

"Why?"

"You have impressed me, Tansy. You are wise beyond your years. Your wit amuses me. I am eager to see what you do with your powers. Together, we cannot be stopped. Not by men. Not even by the gods. Think of it. We will rule forever. Don't you want that? For yourself? Your sister and parents? For your future children."

What is she talking about? "You're wrong about me," I tell her. "I don't have powers of any kind."

"Oh, but you do. They are deep within you. You must first open your mind."

Just give me the stone back so I can leave.

"It's not that easy."

"What do you want from me?" I ask.

"For you to learn the powers and use them. It is the only way."

Let's get this over with. I pretend to go along with it. "Where do I start?"

"With the stone." She holds back her hair to show the chain. "Focus on the stone. See it in your hand. Then truly hold it."

My patience is running out. But I try. I stare at the stone and imagine it in my hand. I close my eyes and see it happen in my mind. For a second I think it might work.

Then something in me snaps. My hands are around her neck. Is this still in my mind? Or is it real? My hand reaches for the chain. I snag the stone.

Her eyes blaze with fury. "You will be sorry for that."

I back away, but she flies toward me. "I will rip your heart out!"

Where's that knight when I need him?

She flings her arm toward me. A surge of power lifts me off my feet. It sends me flying across the room. I hit a wall and fall limply to the floor. In a dazed state, I put the stone into my pocket. My hand feels for the dagger. And I wait for what comes next.

Seconds later, I'm flat against the wall. My arms are pinned. The witch has one hand around my throat. She squeezes tightly. I can hardly breathe. It feels like my eyes will pop out of my head. Her other hand turns into a claw. I watch in horror as she reaches for my heart.

"Witch!" Devin cries out.

Chapter 18

Broken Bonds

The hold on me is broken. I fall to the ground and gasp for air. Devin holds up the glass ball. He and the witch lock eyes.

"My dear Devin," the witch says. "Give the crystal to me."

Devin steps back. He pulls the ball in close to him.

"All right, then. Have it your way," she says. "But I warn you. No good will come of this. Perhaps you should come back to us. Before it is too late."

"I ride for Lord William now. He stands for good, not evil."

She sneers at him. "And I suppose you are here for the girl. You wish to fight for her. Such a knightly thing to do. But is she worthy? I know the truth. About her and about you."

Devin looks down at the ball.

"That's right. The ball holds the secrets. Maybe we should break it. To remind you of your sins."

A strange look comes over Devin's face.

"See the vision I have placed in your mind. The men and women forced to be slaves. All those who were tortured and killed. And for what reason? Marek said they were not worthy of life. And you helped him with his evil deeds."

Devin hadn't told me about any of this.

"Break the ball, Devin. Release the souls. Feel the pain they suffered. Die!"

"You will be the one to die," Devin cries out. "Your power ends now, witch!"

He throws the glass ball at her feet. It shatters into a million pieces. Smoke fills the room.

Devin runs over and pulls me up. He leads me through the room. We stop and look back. Spirits rise in the form of glowing white lights. They moan and cry. I see tears in Devin's eyes.

I look around for Teera. There is no sign of her.

"We must find the escape passage," Devin says. He moves his hands along the wall. At last a door opens.

"What about Teera?" I ask. That's when I hear her voice.

"Tansy!"

"Teera! Where are you?"

"I'm over—"

The witch's screams drown out my sister's voice. I put my hands over my ears and turn to run. That's when I bump into Teera.

Devin grabs my arm. "We must go at once!"

"No!" the witch screams. "I will not die alone!"

Now she is standing in front of us. She flings her arm in our direction. Devin pushes me out of the way. The force misses me and hits Teera instead. A look of shock is on her face. Her lips move to speak. But nothing comes out. She reaches for me.

"Teera!" I take a few steps. I'm close enough to touch her. As I reach out, she starts to fade. I lunge forward but she is gone. I'm on my knees, crying.

Through tears, I watch the witch fade away. Not even the light of a spirit remains.

"We must leave now!" Devin says. He pulls me to my feet.

I don't want to go. My sister needs me.

Chapter 19

Farewell

Devin has to drag me away. He pulls me along through the tunnel to the river. It swells under the heavy rain. A strong current sweeps us away. Lightning flashes in the sky.

Finally we wash up on a bank. The storm is over.

"The witch is dead," Devin says.

"What about Teera?" I ask him. "Is she dead too?"

He bows his head. "I am sorry. I do not know."

We get back to camp. A boy leads us to Lord William. He wants to know that we're safe.

From his tent, we hear haunted screams of terror. They are coming from Merek's castle. Devin and I look at each other. We know what is happening. It is the souls of the dead slaves. Now freed from the glass ball, they are getting even. Merek and his followers won't survive.

The knights are silent. Lord William has ordered them to stay back. They show no signs of happiness.

Yes, they are warriors. It is their job to defend their lord. Killing is part of that. But do they take pleasure in it? I don't think so. There is only the desire to fight for a good cause. And uphold what is right.

I remember how Devin was near tears in the witch's room. I ask him about it.

"I helped some escape," he says. "For that, I was beaten and cast out. I could have done more to help."

I go back to the tent and pull a blanket over my head. But it's not enough to drown out the sounds. They seem to go on forever.

Somehow I manage to fall asleep. When I wake up, there is silence. The horrors that happened behind those walls are over. I close my eyes. Now all I can think about is my sister.

The next morning, Devin comes to the tent. He says that we are moving out. Lord William has declared the city cursed. His men will not enter its gates.

"I can't leave," I say. "I have to find Teera."

"You cannot help her. You must go home."

How can I think of going home without her? What would Mom and Dad say?

"You must go, Tansy." He leads me outside. The light is so bright. It hurts my eyes. "Go home."

I can't move. I'm too afraid. "I don't want to go. I will miss you, Devin."

"I will see you again."

Chapter 20

Home

I open my eyes. The light is so bright. It takes a few minutes to focus. I'm in a bed. The room is not a saloon or a tent or a castle. This place is clean. Everything is white. And it's so quiet. Have I died?

I begin to notice figures in the room. Someone is in a chair, covered by a blanket. Another person is standing by a window.

My head hurts. I reach up to touch it. That's when I hear a voice.

"Tansy?"

My eyes open wide. It's Mom. "Where am I?"

She runs to my side. "You're in the hospital, honey. You were in a coma. It's been three days. We've all been so worried."

"All?"

"Me and your dad and—"

"I'm so sorry, Mom."

"There's no need to be sorry, honey. You're alive. That's all that matters. We can get another car. It's you we can't replace."

I wonder how she can be so cheerful. "Teera," I say sadly. "I lost her."

Mom shakes her head. "No, Tansy. Teera is fine. She has a pretty big bump on her head. But the doctor says it's not serious." Mom pulls back the curtain that's around the next bed. Teera is sitting up. A man is checking her. He must be a doctor.

"Finally," Teera says. "You were asleep forever."

Dad comes over and hugs me. "Welcome back. You scared us."

"We were leaving the library and—"

"Shhh," Dad says. "You'll make yourself sick. Both my girls are here and safe. That's all that matters."

The doctor turns from Teera and smiles at me. "Hello, Tansy. It's nice to finally meet you."

Devin? I look at the name on his ID badge. It says *Devon*. But I'd know those eyes anywhere.

"I'm Devon," he says. "I'm your nurse. How are you feeling?" He checks my pulse. "It's a little fast," he says. "But that's a good sign." He checks my eyes. "Beautiful!"

I feel my face get warm.

Dad walks to the door. "I'll get the doctor."

Teera gets out of bed and comes over to me. She looks at Devin—I mean Devon—and then back at me. She has a grin on her face. It's like she's dying to say something.

I give her my best evil glare. *Please do not embarrass me!*

Dad comes back into the room. A man is with him. He has on a white coat. This must be the doctor. Then I look at his face. Lord William!

"Good morning, young lady. I'm your doctor. My patients call me Dr. Will."

He looks at my chart. Then he examines me. "That was some car accident you had."

Car accident? It was way more than that. I have to explain. They all need to know what happened.

The doctor is speaking to my parents. He's saying something about bed rest. Then he looks at me. "No driving for a while."

"No worries there," I say. I look at Mom. "About the accident. What happened?"

"You don't remember?" she asks.

"Teera was holding the stone. It was flashing in the sunlight. And I grabbed it from her. That's all I remember. Was anyone—"

"No one was killed," Mom says. "Not even the dog

that ran into your path. You swerved in time. But you ran off the road. Some bushes stopped you. Thank God."

"Remember," the doctor says. "No activities until you're fully recovered."

Mom smiles. "Texting will keep her busy." She hands me my phone. "Liv has been calling me like crazy. She's so worried about you."

"I've been worried about her too."

I look at Liv's last message to me. "I'm done with Mark. For good this time!"

"Yay!" I text. "You deserve better. A knight in shining armor."

Devon comes over to me and smiles. *Those eyes!* "Just call if you need anything. Anything at all."

Teera gives me a little smile. "I have something for you."

She holds out her hand. It's the stone.

"You keep it," I say. "Use it for your book report."

"What do you mean?" Teera asks.

"You can tell the class it's magic. It took you back in time. To the Old West. You could even dress up."

"Yeah! Like Wyatt Earp!"

I grin at my sister. We are both okay. It was just a car accident. A bad car accident. Did any of our adventure really happen? I shiver at the thought. The witch had been so real.

Whant to Keep Reading

9781680214772

Turn the page for a sneak peek
at another book in the Monarch
Jungle series.

Chapter 1

Being Kevin Sanders

Kevin Sanders!" people shouted. "I love your videos!"

"Make sure to like and comment," Kevin said. He pushed his hair back and smiled.

Fans held up their phones. He posed for photos.

"Let's go," a man said. He was Kevin's helper. Right now he had one job. Get the star through the crowd.

A path had been roped off. But some fans ducked under it.

"Back!" the man yelled.

"Pipeline," Kevin called. "Come to the booth." He held up his phone. Fans cheered.

Hollywood had film stars. These were online stars. There were dancers and singers. Some wrote books.

Others were bloggers. Many stars gave tips. They were about fashion and makeup.

Their posts got millions of views. It's how regular people got famous. There was a name for it. Instafamous.

Take Kevin. He did pranks. Millions loved his YouTube videos. When he wasn't posting, he was at events. Meeting fans was important.

Today he was at See It Live. It was held once a year in LA. Tickets sold out in minutes. If you were here, you'd made it.

Fans were a big part. But it was also about business. Agents handled that. They made deals. Companies paid stars to use their products. That's how Kevin teamed up with Pipeline Clothing.

They saw a video he made. He was surfing with a shark. Then the video went viral. The company wanted a deal. Ten million people followed Kevin on Instagram. One photo of him sold tons of stuff. In this case, it was surf gear.

Kevin made money too. He got four thousand dollars to be here. His agent set it up. Ron Simon made great deals. Today, the deal was simple. Wear the clothes and pose for selfies.

"Kevin Sanders!" a woman called out. She was a reporter. "What are you working on?"

"Aww. You know I can't say." He gave her a sly grin. "It'll ruin the surprise."

He was working on a show for YouTube. It was called "I am Kevin Sanders."

"Come on, Kev," she said. "Tell us."

"Yeah, Kev," a voice said. "We want to know."

It was Chase Rogers. He was also an online star. Sometimes the two teamed up for pranks.

"What's up?" Kevin said.

"Your shirt," Chase said.

"What about it?"

"It's Pipeline's. They hired me! You're a cheap fake!"

"Don't make me hurt you," Kevin said. He gave Chase a push. Suddenly the crowd rushed in. They started to pull the guys apart. But the two had stepped aside. People hadn't seen them. Now the crowd turned on each other.

Kevin headed for the exit. At the door, he looked back. A fight had broken out. Chase was close behind. They each ran to a limo. Kevin called Chase.

"That was epic!" Kevin said.

"Dude!" Chase said. "Check out YouTube. This thing is blowing up! The traffic's on fire!"

"Doesn't take much, does it?"

"Are you kidding? We started a riot!"